2 stripe

This book should be returned/renewed by the latest date shown above. Overdue items incur charges which prevent self-service renewals. Please contact the library.

**Wandsworth Libraries
24 hour Renewal Hotline
01159 293388
www.wandsworth.gov.uk**

Wandsworth

Also by Nicola Davies:

FICTION

The Heroes of the Wild series

The Silver Street Farm series

NON-FICTION

Animals Behaving Badly

The Animal Science series

ARIKI
and the
GIANT
SHARK

WALKER
BOOKS

First published 2018 by Walker Books Ltd
87 Vauxhall Walk, London SE11 5HJ

2 4 6 8 10 9 7 5 3 1

This book has been typeset in Veronan

Printed and bound in Great Britain
by CPI Group (UK) Ltd, Croydon CR0 4YY

British Library Cataloguing in Publication Data:
a catalogue record for this book is available from the British Library

ISBN 978-1-4063-6979-3

www.walker.co.uk

For Remi and Arlo
and their mummies,
who all love the ocean

Nicola Davies

For Gemma

Nicola Kinnear

We are used to thinking of the sea as something that you get to when the land runs out. But just suppose you lived the other way round, in a place where sea stretched from one horizon to the other and land was very hard to find...

This is not an imaginary place. If you look at a map of the world you can find it, that big expanse of ocean we call the Pacific. A whole world of water dotted with the smallest scraps of land.

Long ago, a girl lived there, on a tiny island shaped like a sea turtle. She rode on the tails of sharks; she used the stars as stepping stones; she sang songs to the storm. But most of all, she knew what it meant to live in the true colour of our planet – which is not green, but blue.

Her name was Ariki and this is one of her adventures.

TURTLE ISLAND

REEF DROP-OFF

DEEP LAGOON

TURTLE BACK BEACH

IPO & GRANNY'S HOUSE

LAGOON

PIG PEN

ARIKI & AROHAKA'S HOUSE

CHAPTER 1

Five sharks circled slowly in the clear water, their shadows tracking over the white sand. Ariki's eyes worked perfectly underwater and so she could see every detail of their bodies, their crescent-shaped fins and the pale shine on their grey skins – these were yellow moon sharks.

She chose the largest, and dived down towards it. She had been diving like this since she could walk, and holding her breath was as natural as blinking, so it was easy to swim gently up behind it. As its tail flapped lazily in front of her, she reached out and closed her fingers around the sandpapery skin. Instantly, the shark jerked in panic; its whole body tensed, and the slow flip-flap of the tail was transformed into a frantic wriggle. Although it was not much longer than one of Ariki's legs, it pulled her along behind it.

The shark shot through the water and did three circuits of the lagoon at high speed before it tired. But by then Ariki, at last, needed a breath. She let go of the shark and swam up to burst through the

surface, laughing. She loved this game, played every year when the baby moon sharks spent their first weeks of life in the quiet and calm of the lagoon. They were too small and inexperienced to be really dangerous, but still big and wild enough to tow any of the island children who were brave enough to hitch a ride. In another month they would learn to turn round and bite, but for now the thought hadn't entered their small shark-brains.

Ariki trod water and considered what to do next. She should swim back to shore and get on with the chores that her guardian Arohaka had left for her to do. But her fishing spear was strapped across her back, ready, and there was just enough daylight left to catch a fish. The chores could wait. She turned from the shore and swam straight out, towards the line of bright, white surf that broke on the crest of the reef. Over the stony, grey wreckage of old coral, broken in storms, and further, to the edge of the lagoon. Beyond was the coral reef, the barrier that ringed Turtle Island, protecting it from the power of the open sea.

The ocean swell spilled over the top of the reef as if it was the lip of a submerged bowl, and poured into the still lagoon. Ariki rode the waves, letting them swoop her back and forth over the reef, the mauves and pinks and yellows of the forest of coral heads and their flocks of fish. It was like flying through a rainbow. She never tired of it ... but now, she needed to hunt! She kicked hard against the incoming waves that threatened to smash her down onto the hard spikes of the coral heads and pushed herself towards open water. For a moment she was engulfed in the chaos of breaking waves and then, quite suddenly, the reef fell away below her, curving down, down, down into bottomless indigo.

Ariki adored this place: the reef drop-off. Corals crowded at its edge. Reef fish swirled in clouds, and big groupers, sharks and barracuda prowled in the shadowy deep, ready to snatch their smaller relatives. Most of all, she loved the sensation of soaring over that great, unknown depth. This was why her chores on land were often left undone: it was only here, alone in the blue, that Ariki felt free.

She took a breath, then dived again. Close to the surface, thousands of orange fish, each one a little smaller than her hand, pressed around her, their shoal opening just enough to let her pass and closing again behind. Their fins brushed her skin and their mouths all made neat little "o"s as they sucked in tiny creatures brought in with the waves. They were not good to eat, however. Ariki was looking for something less bony and bitter tasting.

There! Down among the coral, a malu was pulling a worm out of a hole. Malu were usually common, but this year the rainy season had never come and it had affected the fishing. Tasty fish like this had been hard to find. She must make the most of the opportunity.

Ariki dropped carefully to within range. The malu didn't spot her until it was too late. It wriggled a little on the spear, then was still: it was smaller than it had looked, but it would have to do; she had played for a little too long, the sun was sinking and the deep water of the drop-off was not a safe place to be when night brought the big hunters out of the dark. It was time to swim back to shore.

Then she caught a movement in the water below her, and fear leapt in her belly. She knew that shape, that huge size: it was a nihui, the kind of great fish that her people called the Queen of the Sharks. Nihui were thought to be the most powerful beings in all the ocean. It must have smelled the malu's blood and now it was hungry.

Less than four canoe-lengths away, the shark's great dorsal fin cut the surface as it began to circle. It was an honour to see one, because a nihui could choose to give you some of its power.

Or it could just choose to eat you.

Although her heart was pounding, Ariki knew she must keep calm. A panicked swim for the shore now would only sharpen the nihui's appetite. She took a breath and dived.

It was a young nihui; it still had faint grey stripes on its side and was not full-grown. Still, it was huge, much bigger than a reef shark. As it circled round her, Ariki turned, keeping her eyes on the creature. She watched the muscles ripple under the skin, and saw the teeth, peeping between its partly-opened jaws.

She turned her tattooed left side towards the shark. Tattoos were supposed to protect a person against danger but Ariki had never tried hers out on something quite *this* dangerous. She greeted the shark in her mind, taking care to speak very politely.

Great Nihui, she thought, *you are all powerful, but there is better hunting to be had on Turtle Reef than me. Please take my fish as a token of my respect and let me live!*

She held the malu out on the end of the spear. The nihui paused in its circling and turned its nose towards the fish, holding still in the water. It opened its mouth, just enough to take the fish and snap the spear like a dry twig. Then it circled a little further off and for a moment Ariki believed that her offering had been accepted and her respect acknowledged.

But no. The shark was just taking aim. Its great tail gave one powerful swish and it shot towards her. Its head filled her vision as its jaws began to open; Ariki even saw its eyelids start to close, to protect its eyes as it attacked. The horrible moment stretched, so that she noticed every terrifying detail. She clenched her teeth, braced for the intense pain when the nihui's teeth would slice her in two...

But it did not come, because a vast black shape rammed into the nihui's side, bending it like a leaf.

The nihui floated belly up then sank out of sight as Ariki tumbled backwards through the water.

Confused and spluttering, she struggled to the surface. The sea gleamed pink with the afterglow of the sunset and there was no sign of the nihui's fin, but now there was a much, much bigger fin sticking up above the water – holding still, as if the creature it belonged to was waiting for something. Carefully, she took a breath and put her head under.

Hanging motionless just below the surface to her left was another shark. Although in the dim twilight it was little more than a shape in the water, Ariki could tell that it was at least three times the size of the biggest nihui. If the nihui was the Queen of the Sharks then this was the Empress of Empresses!

Something in its utter stillness told her it wasn't waiting to attack: that it would not harm her. The nihui had radiated nervous energy and anger, but this creature gave out peacefulness. Instead of fear, Ariki felt calm. To be so close to such a giant filled her with wonder; the tattoos on her skin tingled with it. Then, the huge shark's tail beat once, twice ... and in less than a moment it was gone – down, down, down, lost in shadow.

Ariki swam up, gasping for breath. The sea was quiet, as if nothing had happened at all. Who would believe her if she told them that nihui were *not* the most powerful creatures in the ocean? That there was something bigger, more wonderful, and that it had just saved her life?

As she swam back to shore, she could hardly believe it herself!

CHAPTER 2

The next morning, Ariki's punishment for her neg-
lected chores was to clean out the pen of Arohaka's
finest sow, Pupuli. Pupuli was not happy about this.
She was the biggest, angriest pig on the island.
Several people had scars to show from tangles with
her. And right now Pupuli's temper was especially
bad, because a poor harvest had put everyone on
Turtle Island on short rations – including the pigs.
Many islanders were looking hungrily at Pupuli's
piglets and imagining a tasty dinner! But they were
being saved for an important festival to celebrate

the start of the next rains – if they ever came –
when the chiefs of the neighbouring islands would
come visiting.

Pupuli stared at Ariki with her little black eyes.
Get out of my home, get away from my piglets, she
seemed to be saying. But Arohaka had ordered Ariki
to clean out Pupuli's pen, and she was more scared
of her guardian than of a pig with a bad attitude.

"Nice pig," Ariki said in the kindest, calmest voice
she could manage. "*Nice* piggy, *good* piggy."

But Pupuli was neither nice nor good. And she wasn't anybody's "piggy". She made a rumble like a small tornado – and charged. The next thing Ariki knew, she was lying face-down in pig muck, while Pupuli's thirteen piglets ran over her to get to the gate their furious mother had just barged open.

At least she could clean out the pigsty without fear of being bitten by a mad sow. She would round up the naughty piglets and their fearsome mother later... But as Ariki picked herself up and began to fork the pig poo into a big basket, she realized she was being watched. Three children were leaning over the fence behind her – the nieces and nephew of Manatui, the new queen of the island. They seemed to delight in Ariki's troubles.

Tahita was the middle child, skinny and sharp as a pipefish. She was usually the ringleader.

"Oh dear!" She smirked. "Stranger's in trouble *again*!"

"Stranger" was one of the names the island children had for Ariki. She didn't mind; they were right, she *was* a stranger in a way. She hadn't been born on the island but had washed up on the shore as a toddler, her cradle tied to a raft. No one could guess where she had come from. Wherever it was, some people had wanted to send her right back there, but Arohaka had said she was a gift from the ocean – and a gift should never be refused. Ariki was

grateful to her guardian, but as she grew older he seemed less and less pleased with her. She had come to realize that you didn't have to *like* a gift.

"Spotty smells of pig poo!" Tahita's little sister Poa chanted. "Spotty smells of pig poo!"

Ariki rolled her eyes. "Spotty" was another of her island names, given to her because of her tattoos. All children were tattooed to protect them from harm, like a sort of portable magic spell; but Ariki's tattoos

weren't like the swirls and ripples of the Turtle Islanders' tattoos. Hers were complicated patterns of dots and lines. And what the Turtle Islanders found strangest of all was that Ariki was tattooed on the left arm and leg – the "boys' side". Girls were *always* tattooed on the right... Ariki didn't mind her tattoos; they marked her out as different, and she *was* different. She didn't want to spend her time planting things in the gardens with other girls. All she wanted was to be in or on the ocean.

The children hadn't tired of their teasing yet. Balay, the girls' big brother, hadn't had his turn.

"You smell sooo bad!" he said. "But at least we'll be able to find you when you get lost."

He leaned his big, lollopy body over the fence and hissed at Ariki: "Of course *I'll* never be lost *anywhere*, because *I'm* going to be Arohaka's apprentice! One day I'll be a Star Walker!"

Ariki pursed her lips and looked at the ground

until the children walked away. She wouldn't let them see just how Balay's words had stung.

Arohaka was a master navigator, the only one on the island. Almost everyone could find their way to places within a day or so's journey, but only masters could navigate across vast, empty ocean spaces. In his youth, Arohaka had travelled to mountains in the sea that spouted fire, and to islands so big it would take two whole days to walk from one side of them to the other. He held the title "Star Walker" because to steer a course across the ocean, islanders took their direction from the constellations – the patterns the stars made in the sky. Every journey was a path of stars, and the further you went, the more stars you had to know to chart your path. A Star Walker knew thousands and thousands of stars in the sky, as well as every wave and ripple of the sea below.

Ariki longed to learn what Arohaka knew and to wander through that wide, wide world of blue!

Somewhere out there on the ocean was the place she came from – a place where other people carried strange tattoos. If she became a Star Walker, one day she would find it! Arohaka had no children he could pass his knowledge to, so she had always assumed that *she* would be his apprentice.

Would Arohaka really choose Balay instead? Big stupid Balay, who didn't even care about the sea and only wanted to be a Star Walker because it made him sound important.

Was Ariki just Spotty Stranger girl, a gift from the sea that nobody really wanted?

CHAPTER 3

By the time Ariki had carried the very last load of pig manure to the gardens, and rounded up Pupuli and all but two of the escaped piglets, the day was gone. She ran between the coconut palms down to her favourite beach, Neck Cove, and plunged into the sea. The clean salt water took the smell and dirt from her skin at once. Since she had lost the malu to the nihui, she'd had nothing but a few bits of dried coconut all day. It was too dark for spearfishing – and in any case, the nihui had snapped her spear.

But she had another plan.

Ariki pulled a small, battered canoe from its hiding place: under a pile of dead palm – fronds, at the top of the little beach. Before launching it, she struck some sparks from the flint stones she carried in a pouch onto dried grass, to make a little fire. Then she set a few coconut husks glowing inside a large shell. This she balanced on the prow of the canoe, then grabbed her paddle and set off out over the lagoon, over the reef crest and into the ocean.

The light from the glowing coconut husks called to the flying fish. In a normal season it would be quick work to get five or even ten fish skittering onto the deck of the canoe. But since the rains had failed, everything was strange – even flying fish had been hard to come by.

Ariki looked out over the dark sea. It was so calm that the stars were reflected in the smooth surface. She picked out the constellations on the water and in the sky: the Fish-hook, the Chief's Fishing Line, the

Bailer, the Canoe Builder. Even without Arohaka's teaching, she already knew many of the star patterns that people used to find a path across the sea. She bet she knew more than Balay.

The star called the Little Orphan was rising, just peeping over the horizon. If she steered towards that now she would be heading for Manna Atta: Turtle Island's closest neighbour, half a day's journey away. But Little Orphan couldn't take her all the way there. Like all stars, it didn't rise straight in the sky but slanted as it got further from the horizon. So a whole sequence of rising stars was what you needed to keep a true course. Softly Ariki sang:

"Little Orphan
finds a Red Fish,
catches it on the middle of Three Hooks
and with her Little Finger
feeds it to the Leaping Dolphin."

This was how children learnt to remember the list of stars needed to guide you straight to Manna Atta. Each one rose in turn at the same spot on the horizon, so you could keep your course straight through the night and get there before morning. How many more stars would you need to find your way to fire mountains and giant islands – and back again?

Ariki began to sing the song again, and then stopped. As the Little Orphan rose higher there was a new, strange star beside it. Or not exactly a star;

more a sort of glowing blob, as if a neighbouring star had been caught in a raindrop and had begun to dissolve. But the Orphan *had* no close neighbours – that was how it got its name.

Ariki blinked and looked away, then checked again. No, it wasn't something her tired eyes were making up: there *was* a new strange star in the sky! Her heart beat fast. The sky did not change so suddenly; only the moon shrank and grew again, tonight a little bigger than last night. Stars did not appear from nowhere. What could it mean?

Thunk! Thunk! Thunk! Three small flying fish landed in the boat and took Ariki's attention from the sky. Not much of a catch, but still the best in weeks!

As she paddled back to the beach, the moon rose. It showed wisps of smoke drifting over the water ... and a small, familiar figure fanning flames under a leaning palm tree.

Ariki dragged the canoe up the beach and called out to her friend.

"Ipo! You lazy boy!" she teased. "Have you come to eat my fish?"

"I came to catch my own," he replied, "but someone was using my canoe!"

"*Our* canoe!" Ariki corrected him.

"Yes," Ipo agreed, "*our* canoe. Anyway, I hope you caught something to cook on this fire."

Ariki held up her catch, strung on a stick.

"Hmm," Ipo said, "not bad for a girl."

"Any more of that talk and your belly can stay empty!"

Ipo laughed and put his finger to his lips.

He and Ariki had always been friends. One reason was that they were both outsiders. Ipo's parents drowned when he was small, which was why he lived with his granny – but what really set him apart was that he'd been born without any colour in his skin or hair. He was as pale as foam, and could only go outside with his big green parasol to shade him or when the sun was going down. The island children had names for him too: "Bone Boy", "Dead Fish" or just "Ghost". The names never bothered Ipo, they just made him laugh. And that was the other reason why they were friends: Ipo could stay calm in a hurricane, and he was always smiling.

Ariki cleaned the fish, then wrapped one in a leaf for Ipo's granny and the guts in another leaf for Ipo's granny's pig. Ipo cooked the other two fish over the fire. The children pulled the white flesh from the bones with their fingers; there wasn't much of it, but what there was tasted so good!

"Balay thinks he's going to be Arohaka's apprentice," Ariki told her friend.

"Of course he does." Ipo laughed. "He's always been full of himself, the big idiot!"

Ariki wasn't reassured. She threw her fish bones into the fire crossly. "I don't think Arohaka will choose me after all. I don't belong on Turtle Island."

Ipo rolled his eyes. "Don't be silly!" he said. "Just because you weren't born here, doesn't mean this isn't where you belong."

Ariki knew her friend was being kind.

The sky blossomed with stars, and for a long time the only sounds were the crackle of the flames and the sigh of the little wavelets on the shore.

Ipo broke the silence at last. "Want to hear something more exciting than Balay's boasting?" he said.

"Go on then."

"Nihui!" Ipo said. "And not just one – lots of them!"

"Where?" Ariki asked, her heart skipping. All day she'd been wondering if she had imagined last night's encounter, and here was evidence that at least one part of it had really happened!

"Less than a day's journey, off Breadfruit Bank," Ipo replied, his eyes shining with excitement. "Granny says she's never known them to come so close at this time of year!"

Ariki was just about to tell him that they might be even closer than that, when the sound of voices from the Gathering Hut ended their conversation and had them on their feet – and running hard.

CHAPTER 4

The Gathering Hut was the biggest building on the island, with a high roof of criss-crossed timbers covered in palm thatch. It was used for important ceremonies and as a shelter in storms and tornadoes. The rest of the time it was left quiet, to gather spider webs and dust. But tonight its peace was shattered. Lantern light danced on the beams and the air was filled with voices, all talking at once. Even Ipo's granny had made her way there, leaning on her stick.

No one took the slightest notice of Stranger and Bone Boy slipping quietly in through the shadows.

41

At the centre of the excited crowd were Manatui, the queen of the island, and Arohaka. The queen and the Star Walker were supposed to run things together, but they were seldom in agreement about how to do anything. Arohaka had got on well with the old queen, but when she died and her granddaughter became queen the arguments had started. Arohaka thought Queen Manatui was a young hothead and Queen Manatui thought Arohaka was a boring old fool. Right now they were snatching the speaking conch from each other, taking turns to argue back and forth.

"Nihui are sea hunters as we are," Arohaka was saying. "We've lived with them for all time."

Tall and skinny, he stood like a rock, with his mouth a straight, hard line. Short, round Manatui, however, was all sparks and fire, waving her arms about and almost hitting people next to her with the conch.

"This great new beast has come to lead the nihui against us," she cried, her eyes flashing. "Together they threaten our survival!"

"What new beast?" Ipo whispered. "What are they talking about?"

Ariki had a funny feeling she knew, but the arguments were getting too loud to talk over.

Arohaka looked at Manatui as if she was a particularly irritating fly. He pulled the conch out of her hands and cried, "I've never heard such nonsense!"

A queen and a Star Walker were supposed to

treat each other with respect, but not Manatui and Arohaka!

Manatui looked very cross indeed. She yanked the speaking conch back and hissed at Arohaka, "I can prove they're a threat!"

PAAAAAAAP!

Manatui blew a very loud blast on the speaking conch to bring everyone to order.

PAAAAP! PAAAAAAAAP!

It took several loud, trumpeting blasts to make everyone quieten down.

"Brothers! Tell what you saw," Manatui commanded.

The two finest boat-builders on Turtle Island, the twins Ulu and Uku, stepped forward. They were huge, strong men, now the fathers of grown sons – but they still stuck together like glue and always finished each other's sentences, speaking in a sort of relay race.

"We were fishing off Breadfruit Bank," Uku began; the waters off Breadfruit were a favourite spot for big shoals of tuna.

"In our new boat," Ulu went on, "the one with the decking and the two hulls."

People murmured admiringly here; everyone knew about the new boat. It was built to be big enough for days away from land, seaworthy enough to weather storms. Everyone hoped it would bring home a fine catch that would feed the whole island for a month.

"We hooked a tuna," Uku said, continuing the spoken relay, "a *big* tuna ..."

"... a very big tuna ..."

"... the first we've caught for two moons ..."

"... bigger than a man ..."

"... it was on the line ..."

"... hooked! Jumping out of the water ..."

"... and in again."

"When it came up the second time ..."

"... close to the boat ..."

"... very close ..."

"... it had been bitten in half by a nihui."

The crowd stirred a little at this point. But only a little. A big nihui could easily bite a man-sized tuna in half. Most of the older fishers on the island had lost their catches this way at least once.

Uku began again.

"We saw the nihui under the boat."

'There were a *lot* of huge nihui!"

"But when we pulled in what was left of the tuna ..."

"... something big and black ..."

"... like a whale ..."

"... but not a whale ..."

"... pushed the nihui aside and rammed our boat!"

The crowd gasped.

"One hull cracked!" Uku said. He looked so upset Ariki wondered if he was going to cry.

"We patched her up," his brother went on, "to sail home ..."

"... and when we got back ..."

"... we found this, stuck in the wood!"

Ulu held something up to the light. At first Ariki thought it was the axe head, made from a strange dense stone, that Ulu and Uku used for their boat-building. But as the torchlight played on the object, everyone could see what it was: a shark's tooth, bigger than a man's hand. Many men and women wore a shark tooth strung around their necks, as a talisman and a tool. But this tooth was on another scale altogether. As the Turtle Islanders stared at it, they grew very quiet and still, each one imagining the animal to which such a tooth could belong – an animal that was now sharing the waters on which they sailed, in which they fished and swam. Such a creature could bite the biggest boat in two, swallow its crew and still be hungry. It could eat a shoal of tuna, and still want more and more and more.

Manatui took the speaking conch.

"There!" she said, looking around as if she'd just pulled a cooked tuna and a roasted piglet out of the sea. "If attacking a boat isn't a threat, I don't know what is!"

Arohaka's mouth was a tight line – a sign, Ariki knew, that he was furious – but when he tried to take the conch, Manatui swished it sideways and went on, raising her voice to make sure everyone heard.

"It's obvious that this is why the fishing has been so bad! This monster is leading the nihui to eat all our fish!"

Ever since the rains had failed to come, people had been looking for something to blame for their empty bellies, so they were very pleased to hear

this. When Arohaka finally got the conch back and began to speak, everyone was too busy agreeing with Manatui to hear him.

"The sharks aren't *making* the fishing bad, you numbskulls," he raged. "The rains are late, that's what's caused the poor fishing. The seasons are awry. The nihui and this new creature are symptoms, not the disease!"

Now Manatui didn't bother to get the conch; she cried out, "We must hunt this monster!"

"Don't be such a fool!" Arohaka replied. "We don't even know what this creature *is*!"

"I'll tell you what it is," Manatui shouted. "It's a demon, sent to destroy us! There you are! We must kill it before it kills us and eats all our fish!"

Cries of *"Yes"* and *"Right"* and *"Now"* came from all around (mainly from young men with newly sharpened spears).

"Sleep now, Turtle Islanders," Manatui cried, her eyes shining. "Tomorrow we will prepare to hunt the monster!"

Cheering and shouting, the islanders began to dance away with more energy than anyone had had in weeks, leaving just Ipo, Ariki and their elders standing in the dark hut.

"Well," said Ipo's granny, "what a performance!" She prodded Arohaka in the leg with her stick. "Don't let her get the better of you!"

"Huh!" Arohaka grumbled. "She's got everyone behind her. There isn't much I can do!"

"She's cunning, I'll give you that." Ipo's granny chuckled. "She's made everyone forget that her belly is still round while ours are all slapping our backbones!"

"You're right, Granny!" Ipo exclaimed. "How come she's still so fat?"

"Ah!" Granny said with a twinkle in her eye.

"Because she still has breadfruit in her store. And no one will ask her to share it while they're chasing monster sharks!"

She leant on her grandson's arm.

"C'mon, Ipo, I'm tired. Take me home. Come and visit us tomorrow, Ariki."

"I will, Granny!" Ariki smiled.

The old lady turned to Arohaka.

"And as for you, Star Walker," she said, waving her stick at him, "be as brave on land as you used to be on the ocean."

"Easy for you to say, old woman," he growled.

"Easy for you to do, old man!" she cackled, and she tottered away with Ipo, leaving Ariki and her guardian alone.

"Bunch of idiot hotheads!" the old man said. But he sounded sad rather than angry. Sometimes, Ariki felt sorry for her guardian.

Nobody seemed to want to know what he thought these days. Still, it was hard to be sympathetic towards someone who was always so very grumpy.

"Come along, girl!" he croaked. "To bed with you." And he stomped off into the dark.

Ariki trailed behind. She had a lot to think about. First, her giant shark was real! Second, she knew it was a lot closer to Turtle Island than Breadfruit Bank. But she hadn't liked that talk of monsters and killing. Her shark hadn't felt like a threat at all. Should she tell Arohaka this? Would he listen?

She was so busy thinking that she walked right into her guardian, who had stopped on the path to gaze up at the sky.

"Stupid child! Don't you ever pay attention to anything?" Arohaka snapped. "Paying attention is the key to finding your way in the world. You cannot be a Star Walker unless you pay attention. Look! You see that up there?"

Arohaka pointed to where the Little Orphan and the Red Fish hung above the palm tops. The new, fuzzy star had moved! It was beside the Red Fish now, just a little in front, as if heading for the Three Hooks. How could a star move like that?

"Can you see that, girl?" He didn't wait for her answer. "No, of course you can't. There is a new companion for the Red Fish tonight. Ah! The late rains, the nihui, the giant beast, this star – they are part of a new path. If we only pay attention, we might see where we're going."

Ariki wanted to say how she'd already seen the new star, and that it was in a new place tonight – but she knew Arohaka wouldn't believe her. So she said nothing and let him scold her all the way home.

"Two piglets still missing, I see," he said as they reached the house. "You'd better find them tomorrow or there'll be trouble! Now get along to bed."

CHAPTER 5

Ariki lay on her sleeping mat, listening to the sea.

Sssssshhhhhhhhh! Sssssshhhh! it whispered, in tiny wavelets that crept up the beach outside Arohaka's house. Without opening her eyes she could tell that it was another day of glassy calm, heat and clear sky. Another day when the rains wouldn't come. Arohaka was wrong. She *did* pay attention. She *did* notice things. He just didn't want to listen!

Well, maybe he'd listen if she found those two missing piglets. Ariki opened her eyes and smiled. She gave a big stretch then jumped up. She was pretty sure she knew where they'd be.

But when she got to Pupuli's pen, the missing piglets were not back in with their mother. There was no sign of them anywhere. It was odd: they were still suckling so they should be very hungry by now and eager to come home. She glanced around, wondering if they were close by and just startled by her presence.

A gang of small children was poking around under the trees. They were most likely looking for robber crabs unwise enough not to have run for their burrows as soon as it was light. Robber crabs were very tasty, if you could catch one without it chopping off a finger or two with its claws.

The children were very skinny – the littlest children were always the first to show it when food was scarce. They looked back at Ariki from under tangles of hair. They had a guilty look about them.

"Why are you staring at us?" one asked.

"I'm looking for help," Ariki said, smiling. "Help to find Arohaka's missing piglets."

The children bunched together like startled fish and studied their dirty toes.

"I don't suppose," Ariki asked, innocently, "that any of *you* have seen them, have you?"

She came closer to the knot of children. One or

two of them looked ready to bolt. One or two looked ready to cry.

The smallest, a little boy, broke down and began to snivel. "We were *so* hungry!" he wailed. "And it tasted *so* good!"

Now they were all snivelling, terrified that scary Stranger would tell on them. Ariki bit her cheeks so as not to laugh.

"Quieten down now," she told them. "D'you want the whole island to hear what you did?"

They shook their heads; Ariki leaned in close.

"Did you eat both the piglets?" she asked.

They shook their heads again.

"D'you know where the other one is?"

The children all looked towards a taller, slightly stronger-looking child – "Pilo", he was called.

"We saved it. For later," Pilo whispered.

"If you show me where," Ariki said, "then I promise I won't tell."

The children looked at each other, then at Ariki. Pilo nodded.

"Follow us!" he said, suddenly cheerful. "We'll show you!"

And they tore off, like so many wild piglets themselves.

They were small and fast and knew their way far better than Ariki, who had spent very little time in the green thickets that covered the heart of Turtle Island. She had always been far more interested in the ocean than the land. When the children finally stopped leading her between trees and under bushes, Ariki was in a place she'd never seen before.

"There!" said Pilo.

"Where?" She looked to where the small boy pointed: a tangle of palms growing over and between a tower of huge, grey boulders.

"In there!" the children chorused.

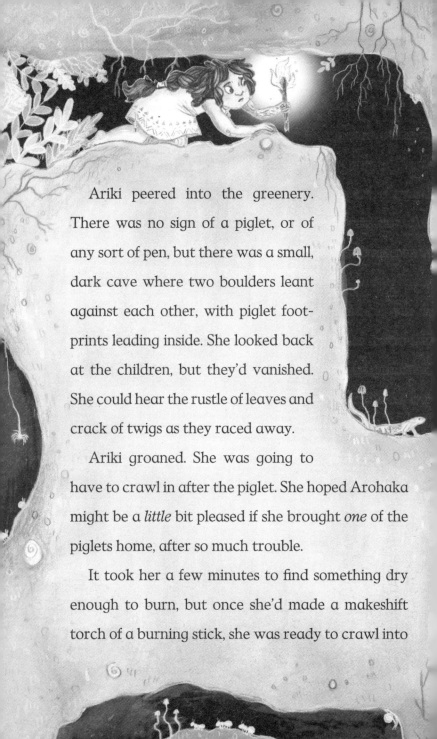

Ariki peered into the greenery. There was no sign of a piglet, or of any sort of pen, but there was a small, dark cave where two boulders leant against each other, with piglet foot-prints leading inside. She looked back at the children, but they'd vanished. She could hear the rustle of leaves and crack of twigs as they raced away.

Ariki groaned. She was going to have to crawl in after the piglet. She hoped Arohaka might be a *little* bit pleased if she brought *one* of the piglets home, after so much trouble.

It took her a few minutes to find something dry enough to burn, but once she'd made a makeshift torch of a burning stick, she was ready to crawl into the hole. It was deep! Ariki had expected to find a canoe-length of tunnel with the piglet at the end of it, but it went much further. All sorts of island creatures were hiding out in here: beetles, spiders, small green geckos and young robber crabs.

The tunnel twisted and turned but did not branch, and round one sharp corner she found the piglet. It was clearly the runt of the litter but was doing just fine away from mum. Island pigs learned to eat anything and this little piggy was munching up the remains of a small robber crab, and looking full of life. So full, that it took one look at Ariki and took off down the tunnel at top speed. With a sigh, she went after it.

The roof got so low that Ariki had to wriggle on her belly, but faint daylight showed up ahead, giving enough light for her to leave the torch behind. After a little more squeezing, Ariki could see the tunnel opened out a bit further on. Something there was moving, making shadows flicker on the rock up ahead... The piglet, at last!

Ariki braced her feet on the walls and shoved hard. Her head popped out into a chamber, just large enough for two people to sit upright. To her left the piglet stood against the wall; but right in front of her, the biggest robber crab she had ever seen waved its massive claws a hand's breadth away, ready to slice her face in two. Ariki could do nothing with her arms pinned beneath her but before the crab could snap its claws, a small, spotted missile knocked it flying. The piglet had charged and sent the crab rolling over the rocks to the other side of the chamber. The crab decided flight was better than fight,

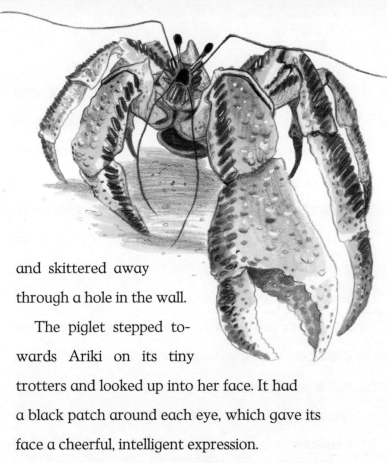

and skittered away
through a hole in the wall.

The piglet stepped to-
wards Ariki on its tiny
trotters and looked up into her face. It had
a black patch around each eye, which gave its
face a cheerful, intelligent expression.

"I think I owe you a favour,
piggy," Ariki told it, and
scratched the top of its
head. The piglet wiggled
its corkscrew tail and
blinked with pleasure.

"All right," Ariki laughed. "Come with me and I'll do my best to make sure you don't end up as anyone's dinner just yet! I'd better give you a name. How about Bad Boy?"

The piglet gave a small grunt of approval.

The route that the crab had used was too small for a person, but crawling back down the tunnel clutching a piglet – even a willing one – wasn't going to be much fun. Ariki scooped up Bad Boy and looked around for another way out.

The dim greenish light let in by the crab's escape route showed there *was* no other exit. It also showed something far more interesting. The rock walls and ceiling were covered in pictures, scratched deep into the stone. Although the animals and people in them were drawn very simply, just outlined shapes, they were so full of life that Ariki could imagine them moving across the stone and out into the world. Some were too worn to see clearly, some were half covered with green mould, but the biggest – those that covered the curved roof above her – were clearest.

The first picture showed a crowd of nihui and another much, much larger shark. The big shark was pregnant, with several pups clearly carved inside her belly. But it didn't look to Ariki as if this "monster" shark was leading the nihui at all. Their teeth were bared and they surrounded the big shark so she couldn't escape. It looked to Ariki as if they were waiting to eat the baby sharks that were about to be born. The giant shark could defeat one nihui – Ariki had seen it happen – but not a whole gang.

The next picture showed two boats, just like the boats the islanders used every day for fishing, with four people in each one. A huge net was stretched in the water between the boats. But it wasn't catching any fish. Instead it was a barrier, with the big pregnant shark on one side and the hungry nihui on the other. On either side of the boats were two long thick lines: Ariki puzzled over these. There was

something about the shape they made that was familiar, but she couldn't quite see what.

It was the last picture that really took Ariki's breath away. This showed the shark with her newborn pups swimming free beside her. Above, the artist had carved the constellations of the night sky: the Little Orphan, the Red Fish, the Three Hooks and the Leaping Dolphin. All the stars were carved as little holes in the stone – except one, which was a small irregular circle, a fuzzy blob, just like the new star Ariki had seen, but in a slightly different place from where it had been last night, and the night before.

Ariki reached up and traced the scratched pictures over and over again with her fingertip. How old were they? Too old for anyone living now to know they were here. Too old probably for even Ipo's granny's granny to have told anyone about them. And yet they showed that it had all happened before: the new star, the gathering of the nihui and the giant shark. Now the giant shark had come back, not to take their food or attack their boats, but to ask for their protection while she gave birth to her young! Here was the path Arohaka had talked of – not a *new* path but an *old* one.

Bad Boy seemed to understand that the journey back through the tunnel was necessary and didn't wriggle, so the scramble to the outside wasn't too bad. With her new friend trotting at her heels, Ariki set off through the greenery to Turtle Back Beach.

CHAPTER 6

Most islanders lived along Turtle Back Beach and kept their boats pulled up under the trees there. Small canoes could be launched almost anywhere on the island, to fish in the lagoons inside the reef or cross the top of the reef to get to open water. But launching bigger boats could only be done from Turtle Back, because the reef there had a break in it – a narrow channel that the islanders called the Nose. Even at the lowest tides the Nose had enough water in it to allow the big tuna-fishing boats, like Ulu and Uku's, to get out to the ocean. Turtle

71

Islanders always said, "Without our Nose we cannot breathe!" – meaning, without the channel to the open ocean, fishing and travelling would be difficult.

Turtle Back was special in another way too. The reef enclosed a huge, deep lagoon, the envy of all the neighbouring islands. It was a perfect place for children to learn boat-handling and swimming. It usually held a nice supply of tasty food, too, like flatfish and sea cucumbers; although now, with food scarce in other places, these had all been gobbled up.

Ariki was making for Ipo's granny's house, which was right in the middle of the curve of Turtle Back. Ipo's granny was too old to do much except lie in her hammock and gossip, so she'd had a big shady roof built over the flat sand to one side of her house. This was a great place to stand around and chat: Granny was never short of news or company.

It was also Ipo's workspace. Ipo might be Bone Boy, Dead Fish or Ghost to some, but his designs of birds and fish, leaves and trees covered everybody's best clothes. With his bone pen, and ink made from soot, he transformed plain bark-cloth garments into something beautiful. People even came from other islands to get him to decorate their outfits, or to make a picture to mark a special event.

Usually at this time in the morning Turtle Back would be quiet: the cane blinds that made the house walls would be rolled up to let in the air, there would be a smell of roasting breadfruit or cooked fish, and the blue of the sea and the white of the sand would be dotted with islanders making a gentle start to the day. Ipo would be at work in the shade with his pens, chatting to someone as they stretched and yawned.

But as soon as Ariki stepped out of the trees and onto the sand, she could see that the only normal thing about the day was that Ipo's granny was in her hammock. Everything else was most definitely *not* usual. The whole of Turtle Back was huddled under the shady roof, staring out to sea and making worried mumblings. Ariki slipped in between them and stood next to Ipo.

"What's going on?" she whispered.

"Take a look!" he said, and pointed to where everyone was staring. Just where the Nose led out into the ocean, twenty or more big shark fins were cruising back and forth. Closest to the entrance to the Nose, the biggest fin of all sliced the water one way and then the other: a vast black crescent, like the front of a huge canoe.

A young mother called Baha, with a sleeping baby on her back, was the first to say what people were thinking.

"They're blocking off the Nose so we can't go fishing!"

"Yes," said her husband, "they want us trapped!"

More and more people added their voices, each one sounding more agitated than the last.

"They want to keep all the fish for themselves!"

"They want us to be afraid!"

"They want us to starve!"

"They want to kill us!"

"Yes! Yes! They do!"

The worried mumblings had grown to cries and shouts and now Manatui was coming out of her house a little further down the beach. It was just like everyone else's but she liked to call it "The Palace", and had got Balay and his sisters to surround it with rows of sunbleached shells. She had put on her best tunic, the one she'd had Ipo decorate with a rising sun. And she was carrying the speaking conch, which showed that she had Something Important to Say.

People were too busy watching the black fins to take any notice of her approach, so she gave a blast on the conch and began to shout as she bustled down the beach.

"Now is the time to sharpen our spears!" she cried. "We can end our hunger, end our troubles, if we fight these creatures!"

But she wasn't the only one hurrying towards the crowd. Arohaka came stomping out of the trees. His hair was tied into a knot on the crown of his head, the way warriors wore their hair in battles, and he

carried a huge spear. *Where has the old rogue been hiding that?* Ariki wondered. She'd never seen it before. It certainly worked to get people's attention: no one was looking at Manatui now. This wasn't grumpy old Arohaka, who squabbled with the Queen and called her names; this was their Star Walker who understood the great secrets of the sky and ocean!

"This spear," Arohaka said, his eyes dancing, "is made from the teeth of the sperm whale. I brought it, in my youth, from the islands where fire shoots from high land. It can kill *anything*. It can kill giant sharks."

Manatui's mouth was open but no words came out. Everyone else stared, wide-eyed.

"I am not afraid to die," Arohaka cried. "I am not afraid to kill. But nihui and this new beast are creatures of great power, creatures to respect. To kill without reason offends the ocean that gives us our life."

Manatui found her voice again. "There *is* reason! They have taken our fish!"

Ariki could see Arohaka struggling not to call the Queen an idiot or a numbskull, but he kept his voice calm and determined.

"And the rains and the crops?" he asked. "Have the great sharks taken those too?"

Manatui gave a little toss of her head.

"Yes! Yes!" she said, sounding like a child having a tantrum. "They have eaten the clouds, eaten the rains. The ocean has sent them here for us to kill!"

Arohaka drew himself up very tall and straight. "Then," he replied, "let us see who's right. You and I, Manatui, will go to sea right now! If the nihui and the giant beast attack our boat, then I will be the first to cast a spear."

Manatui looked horrified. She hadn't thought that *she* would be going out in a boat among the sharks! That was someone else's job. But like Ipo always said, she was clever.

"You are wasting time, Arohaka," she said. "Everyone here believes that the sharks threaten us, that we should attack now. We should fill a boat with our strongest fighters, our surest spears. Not with *old men*."

She turned and looked slowly round the islanders. "Is there anyone here who believes these sharks are *not* our enemies? Is there anyone here who does not fear the giant beast?"

People looked at their feet. A moment before, Arohaka had pulled the crowd his way; now, like the backwash of a wave, they were swept back to Manatui.

The pictures in the cave sprang into Ariki's mind: the two boats with the net between and the sharks enclosed by two fat lines. Suddenly she knew what those lines were: they were the edges of the Nose. The picture showed the giant shark trying to swim through the channel and reach the lagoon.

If only everyone could see that picture they would understand that the big shark wasn't a monster, but just a mother looking for safety, being bullied by predators. A creature asking for their help, deserving their protection. But there wasn't time for that now. There was just one way she could protect the great shark from Manatui and her angry talk.

"Here," Ariki whispered to Ipo, "take care of my pig. He's called Bad Boy. Don't let anyone eat him."

"Why? What are you going to do?"

Before she could answer him, her feet had taken her into the space in front of the crowd and the words had left her mouth.

"I do not fear the giant shark!" she cried. "I will swim with the giant shark to prove it is no threat to us!"

Ariki had to admit that the looks on both Manatui and Arohaka's faces were almost worth risking her life for.

"I have swum with her before," she announced, "and I know she means us no harm."

All around her people were exclaiming and looking at the Stranger girl with the boy's tattoos, the girl who had come out of the sea from some mysterious place far away. It was as if they'd never seen her before. Only Balay was unimpressed.

"Stranger's going to be fish food," he hissed as she passed. "That giant shark will snap you up!"

As usual, Ariki ignored him. It wasn't the giant shark that worried her, anyway. It was the nihui. She already knew that, no matter how much respect you showed them, they were still just hungry.

CHAPTER 7

It was decided that they would use Ulu and Uku's other boat, and take some of the strongest spear-throwers as Manatui had suggested. Arohaka didn't fight this compromise. In fact he hardly said anything at all while they got the boat ready. He refused to even look at Ariki. "Probably thinks I was lying about swimming with the giant shark," she said to herself.

Arohaka wasn't the only one who was cross.

"Why didn't you tell me about the giant shark?" Ipo asked, as they sat together in the shade while the crew rushed to get their best spears and find their totem necklaces for good luck.

Ariki tried to explain, but it was hard. "At first, I thought I might have imagined it. I wasn't really sure until today. And then there just wasn't time to say anything."

Ipo still looked hurt.

"I was coming to tell you about it this morning," Ariki went on. "I found out something else too..."

But Ulu was calling to her – the boat was being pushed into the water, Manatui was already sitting on board and everyone was running down the beach. It was time to back up her words with action.

Ariki patted Bad Boy's head.

"If I don't come back, don't let anyone eat this piglet! And get Pilo to show you where they hid him. It'll explain everything."

Ipo's pale eyes were full of questions that there was no time to answer. Ariki trusted that the pictures in the cave would do that, if the nihui made a meal of her.

The sea was calm, just as it had been for weeks. But today it was something more: tense, like a length of spider silk stretched to breaking. As they moved out over the lagoon towards the Nose, the horizon began to blur and the first mist anyone had seen for months began to gather. It cut out the warmth and light of the sun, and turned the sea from bright blue to dark jade.

There were three paddlers in each of the boat's two hulls: Ulu and Uku; three of Ulu's oldest sons; and Mattay, the tallest, strongest woman on the island, who could throw a spear further and harder than any man. They breathed together as they picked up speed. Arohaka stood in the stern behind Ulu. Manatui perched in the middle of the platform, hanging on so hard her knuckles were pale. No one said a word – but Ariki felt their eyes on her as she sat on the edge of the platform, her legs dangling as they flew over the sea.

She tried hard to think of the calm that had surrounded the giant shark, and of the pictures on the wall of the cave. But Balay's voice saying, *"Stranger's going to be fish food!"* played over and over in her head. What had she done? Whatever made her think that the giant shark had rescued her on purpose? It was all some strange coincidence. And now she was going to be snapped up, just like Balay said. She would never get to be a Star Walker and find out where she'd come from.

Uku called for the paddlers to hold the boat back just a little, so they could ride the backwash down the Nose and out to the deep water where the sharks were patrolling. The boat dropped and rose on the swell, then the paddles worked the water to a foam. In a few heartbeats they had popped through and out over the drop-off, where the water went straight down to the very depths – to the bottom of the world.

"Hold position here!" Arohaka commanded. "If they mean us harm we'll soon know it."

In spite of the stillness of the water, there were currents moving under the taut surface. The paddlers' muscles bulged and strained as they held the boat in place. And cutting through the dark sea all around were the fins of the nihui. Ariki counted them: twenty-three at the surface at once, perhaps more beneath.

"Keep a lookout," the old Star Walker ordered. "Whatever happens, we must be ready!"

Manatui, Ariki noticed, didn't say a thing. She

looked rather pale.

The veil of mist began to shut them in, making small sounds seem louder – the water rushed back and forth through the Nose behind them, the timbers of the boat creaked and the fins of the nihui swished.

Slowly, slowly, the minutes passed. To and fro the fins went, round and back ... round and back, but they came no closer.

"They are taking no notice of us," Arohaka observed.

"You'll eat your words when their leader comes," Manatui snapped.

Then, as if something had ordered it, the fins disappeared. Everyone on the boat stared down, trying to see if the nihui were under the boat. But they had vanished.

As they peered into the water a huge patch of darkness grew under the surface, a few canoe-lengths away. It was as if a cloud had formed in the sea instead of the sky, gathering like a storm. Then this fuzzy blackness came rushing to the surface, rushing towards them, gathering speed – and they could all see it was a shark: a huge, vast, enormous, *giant* shark!

Everyone was shouting. Arohaka stood with his spear poised, shouting at the crew to hold the boat steady. Manatui was shouting at Arohaka, telling him to use his spear, now! Uku was shouting at the oarsmen to get the boat out of the way. And then everyone was shouting at Ariki, wanting to know if the great shark was talking to her.

Ariki didn't hear them; as soon as the dark shape had shown itself, the sound of human voices faded. The shouting that grew around her no longer seemed important. The tattoos on her left arm and leg had begun to tingle so much that Ariki looked at them, half expecting them to hover above her skin. She let go and slid into the water with hardly a splash, right into the path of the giant shark.

It was a relief to be underwater. It was calm down here. The hazy light from the misty sky penetrated the sea in pale pleats. Far above, at the surface, was the shape of a boat, dwarfed by the shapes of the nihui, swimming under it but too deep for their fins to break the surface.

Ariki couldn't decide if she was sinking or diving. It didn't seem to matter. Down, down, down she went, and beside her all the way, *she* came: the shark. *Her* shark!

The giant shark bumped Ariki with her nose, and opened her mouth to show rows of teeth, each one bigger than a man's hand. But Ariki was not afraid. Her tattoos were singing and she was once again filled with a great sense of peace. She drifted along the side of the shark, like a piece of weed. Above her its gill-slits flapped and billowed, big as palm fronds moving in a wind.

And then, there was one of the shark's eyes, so black, like a porthole into the starless regions of the night sky – into which Ariki tumbled...

She swam in the creature's mind, soaking up some of its thoughts, feeling them like currents with different speeds and temperatures. She was called "Wahine" – or that was the nearest Ariki could get to the naming-thought that flowed around her. Wahine: an old word for queen or lady. And Wahine *was* old – so, so old. She had lived longer than twenty human lifetimes, more perhaps. She knew the cycles of the ocean, the great currents that ran in the deeps and brought years of calm and years of storms. Seasons as giant as the shark herself, that ran for decades, peaks and troughs of plenty, blooms of life and death. Now was the peak of a long, long season, a time that came just once in hundreds of years, when ocean currents, stars and moon all aligned, so the giant shark could have her babies!

The shark's big, slow thoughts rose through Ariki's mind like a tide.

When the Dolphin gets a yellow eye, Wahine's mind said, *and the ocean grows, I will swim through the tunnel to the pool to make my birthing. Humans must help. Humans will help!*

Ariki fell from the shark's eye and the great creature swam away, down deep, closer to the world's heart.

Oh, Ariki thought calmly. *I wonder if I'm drowning.*

CHAPTER 8

Somebody was leaning on her ribs, pumping them down-up, down-up, down-up. It was an odd sensation. Ariki wasn't sure she liked it and was about to swim off back into the darkness when her body remembered to breathe. She rolled over and was sick, then rolled back and opened her eyes.

"Ah! She's alive!"

It was Arohaka who had been pressing on her ribs and it was Arohaka who was smiling, *smiling* at her now. He was clearly very pleased indeed that she was alive. So too was Ipo, who Ariki now saw

was crouched beside her, shaded by his parasol of leaves. Somehow he managed to look even paler than normal.

Other faces looked down too: Manatui, Ulu and Uku, Balay. The whole island was pressing in, their whispers lapping around Ariki's head.

"She swam with the great shark..."

"No she didn't, she just fell in..."

"I think it spoke to her..."

"We should have put her back on the raft when she was a baby!"

"Perhaps the shark has a message for us..."

She didn't really hear anything they were saying because Wahine still filled her mind. She wanted to tell everyone about the shark's thoughts. To say them out loud, so people would know that the giant shark meant no harm, that she was returning to Turtle Island for a wonderful reason – that she needed their help. But Ariki felt almost too weak to keep her eyes open. Moving her lips was as much as she could do. Arohaka noticed and leant close while she breathed the words the giant shark had put in her head.

"The great shark Wahine, she says when the Dolphin gets a yellow eye and the ocean grows, she will swim through the tunnel to the pool to make her birthing. Humans must help. Humans will help!"

Arohaka looked at her as if he was staring down

to her bones. Then he nodded and smiled.

"Rest now," he whispered kindly. "Rest! You have done well."

Ariki shut her eyes and sighed. She didn't see or hear as the old man straightened up and repeated the shark's thoughts. Everyone was mystified; what could the strange words mean? Manatui was ready to make the most of their uncertainty.

"What nonsense!" she cried. "The meaningless ravings of a child!"

Arohaka shook his head. "No! I think they have an important meaning."

"What meaning?" Manatui demanded.

The people held their breath, waiting for Arohaka to share some great secret, but he only sighed.

"I don't know yet."

Manatui gave a sly smile, and lifted her voice to speak to the islanders.

"*I* know what it means," she said. "It means

Arohaka is wrong. The shark *is* our enemy. The Stranger girl did not swim with the giant, she fell in and was rescued by her guardian. The rest of us only just escaped from the monster demon shark with our lives!"

Arohaka tried to explain how the shark had dived under their hull without even touching it, how the nihui had simply disappeared from sight and how the biggest threat had been Manatui almost capsizing the boat by running about the deck in a panic. But no one wanted to hear.

"I, your Queen," Manatui announced grandly, "will send word to our sister island, Manna Atta. By tomorrow morning we will have more boats, more spears – enough to make war on this great shark that threatens us!"

The whole village streamed away down the beach behind Manatui, singing and shouting in excitement.

Ariki felt Arohaka pick her up and begin to walk.

She heard Ipo's footsteps padding alongside as the old man carried her across the island to their home. And then she knew she must be dreaming, because her guardian said, "I have not paid enough attention to this child that the sea gave us. I thank the ocean and the great shark for returning her to me."

Then a dream of Ipo said, "I found something by following one of your pigs, Star Walker!"

Ipo would never follow a pig, and in any case, how would you find anything that way?

What a silly dream, Ariki thought, and sank back into the dark.

CHAPTER 9

A small rubbery nose poked into Ariki's ear and woke her. Bad Boy stared into her face and shook his head so his ears flapped. Ariki reached out and scratched the piglet's head while her brain slowly came back from wherever it had been.

Outside the hut, silhouetted against the evening sky, sat Arohaka and Ipo, looking at a bark cloth by lantern light. Shakily Ariki tottered over with Bad Boy at her ankles and sat down beside them.

"I think you need to rest more," Arohaka growled.

"I think I don't," Ariki replied.

Arohaka gave a small smile.

"What are you both looking at?" Ariki asked.

Ipo tapped the barkcloth.

"As soon as you got in the boat I went to find Pilo," Ipo explained. "I crawled down that horrible tunnel and drew what I found."

The barkcloth showed a perfect copy of the rock pictures from the tunnel.

"This tells the whole story," Ariki cried, already feeling much better. "It shows it's all happened before, and that the great shark comes here to have her babies. We just need to show this to everyone and—"

But Arohaka interrupted her. "It's too late," he said, shaking his head. "No one will believe what these pictures say now. We are three people against two whole islands!"

Ariki looked from Arohaka to Ipo. Both their faces were dark as clouds.

"What do you mean, 'two whole islands'?"

Ipo put his hand on her arm. "Ariki, Manatui has sent messengers to Manna Atta," he told her. "Tomorrow morning their boats will get here with many spears to kill the great shark and the nihui."

The people of Manna Atta loved to fight. They were always looking for an excuse to use their sharpened spears.

"No!" Ariki wailed. The thought of Wahine's request for help being met with boatloads of warriors was more than she could bear.

"The great shark and her kind may have been coming here since the world began," Arohaka sighed miserably, "but Manatui wants an enemy to make her look like a great leader."

He seemed defeated; there was no sign of the Star Walker who had marched across the island with his great spear only that morning.

"But what about the new star?" Ariki cried. "There, in the picture and in the sky. Isn't that proof? I saw it the night I first saw Wahine."

"You saw this star?" Arohaka said, sitting up a little straighter.

Ariki nodded.

"Why didn't you say so when I pointed it out?"

Ariki looked down at the piglet snuffling at her feet.

"You wouldn't have listened," she whispered. "And it was in a different place, next to the Little Orphan. So I wondered if I was right, because a star can't move, can it?"

There was a sudden gleam in her guardian's eye. "No," said Arohaka. "But a comet can."

Ipo, who had been studying the pictures, raised his head. "What is a comet?"

"It is a traveller among the stars," Arohaka explained. "It comes to our sky, then wanders for a hundred lifetimes, and then comes back. It signals some change in the world. Perhaps the end to a season of poor fishing and no rains. Hmm." The old man rubbed his forehead as if trying to make the thoughts inside speed up. "Tell me again," he went on, "what the – what Wahine said, Ariki."

Ariki shut her eyes and summoned the thoughts of the shark.

"When the Dolphin gets a yellow eye and the

ocean grows, I will swim through the tunnel to the pool to make my birthing. Humans must help. Humans will help!"

"Is the comet the yellow eye?" Ipo asked.

"Yes, I think it is!" said Arohaka. He began to smooth a place on the sand with his palm.

"Hold the lantern, Ipo, so I can see," he ordered. He murmured Wahine's words over and over – "When the Dolphin gets a yellow eye... When the Dolphin gets a yellow eye..." and he began to draw constellations in the sand. "Here is the Little Orphan,

next the Red Fish, then the Three Hooks and the Dolphin."

Ariki and Ipo nodded eagerly.

"Ariki, when you first saw the comet," Arohaka went on, "where exactly was it?"

Ariki pointed to the spot next to the Little Orphan.

"Two nights ago it was here."

"And last night it was here." Arohaka pointed just a little in front of the Red Fish, then measured the distance between the two positions with his fingers.

"So from one night to the next it travels this far," he said.

Ipo gasped. "That means tonight it will be as far on again!" he cried. "Which takes it next to the Dolphin!"

Ariki leapt to her feet.

"Tonight is when the Dolphin gets a yellow eye and Wahine has her babies!"

She wanted to leap into the air. With luck, Wahine would have her pups before the Manna Atta boats arrived, and swim away at once and be safe. The pups would be living proof that Manatui had been wrong all along about the great shark's reason for coming to Turtle Island. But they didn't have much time. It was already dark.

"Come on!" she said to Ipo. "We need to find two boats and a big net."

But Ipo was staring at the bark picture and frowning.

"It looks as if the net is to keep the nihui away from Wahine, but a net wouldn't stop nihui," he said. "And what does the ocean growing mean?"

Ariki was about to scold Ipo for wasting time, but Arohaka the Star Walker was on his feet now, his back straight and his head held high.

"Sometimes, Ipo, we must take action without knowing what will happen," he said gently. "All we can do is what this picture and Wahine have told us. Ariki's right, we need two boats and a net ..."

"The biggest we can find," Ariki added.

"... and lots of pairs of hands," Arohaka concluded. "But thanks to Manatui, I expect they will have to be very small ones!"

CHAPTER 10

Arohaka estimated that the Dolphin constellation would appear when the night was almost over. If they were right, then as the Dolphin rose the comet would move into position and the predictions of the stone pictures and the great shark's words would come true. Wahine would be gone just before dawn.

But if they weren't right... Ariki tried not to think about the boats from Manna Atta, already on their way over the dark ocean, full of angry men with spears and empty bellies.

Arohaka, Ipo and Ariki had divided the night's

tasks between them. Arohaka was organizing boats, Ipo was finding a net and Ariki had to find the "pairs of hands". All of it had to be done in secret, in case Manatui and her supporters tried to stop them – which was why Ariki was creeping around the outside of one of the houses at Turtle Back, trying to work out where Pilo slept. The end wall of the house was rolled up to let the sea breeze in, but it was impossible to tell which of the sleeping shapes inside was Pilo.

Bad Boy gave a small grunt.

"Shhh!" Ariki told him.

But the piglet grunted again and tapped Ariki's foot with one small trotter, trying to get her attention.

"Stop it!" Ariki scolded. "I haven't got any food for you now. Shhh."

Bad Boy gave up trying to communicate with Ariki and simply took off into the house, slipping between the sleeping bodies and disappearing into the shadows. A moment later, to Ariki's astonishment, the piglet reappeared, followed by Pilo. Ariki put her finger to her lips and led the small boy down the beach away from the houses.

"Are we going to eat the piglet?" Pilo asked eagerly.

"No," Ariki replied.

Pilo's little face looked up at her, hopeful and a bit puzzled in the starlight.

Ariki realized she hadn't really thought about how she would get Pilo to help. There was no point telling him anything other than the truth.

"I need your help, and your friends' too. We're going to help the giant shark have her babies, so she'll go away and not give us any trouble."

"Oh!" said Pilo. "That sounds exciting. *Then* can we eat the piglet?"

"No, but I think there might be a big feast. And I promise I'll catch some fish for you and your friends."

"My dad says you're really good at fishing,"

115

Pilo commented, "but a bit weird too."

Ariki decided this was quite a good description of her overall, but it wasn't getting them very far. "So, will you help?"

Pilo put his head on one side, suddenly looking older than he was. "It's a big secret, this, isn't it?"

Ariki nodded.

"Good!" Pilo grinned. "I like secrets."

"Can you get about eight of your friends to come to Neck Cove as soon as you can – really fast?"

"What's eight?"

Ariki held up her fingers and Pilo nodded.

"OK."

"Really quickly and really, really quietly."

Pilo put his finger to his lips and took off running down the beach, fast and light as a leaf in the wind.

Ariki stepped out of the shadows onto the crescent of sand at the cove. The remains of the fire on which she and Ipo had cooked the flying fish were a dark circle on the pale shore. That had been just two nights ago. It seemed like years. Ariki looked around; there was no sign of Ipo or Arohaka. No sign of anything or anyone, but up above, the Little Orphan, the Red Fish and the Three Hooks were already high in the clear sky. The Little Finger would soon peep above the horizon, and then the Leaping Dolphin. Time was running out.

Ariki scanned the sea. No sign of sharks, just that
unusual calm. The horizon was tight as a drum and
it felt to Ariki as if the ocean was holding its breath,
waiting for something. The sound of paddling drew

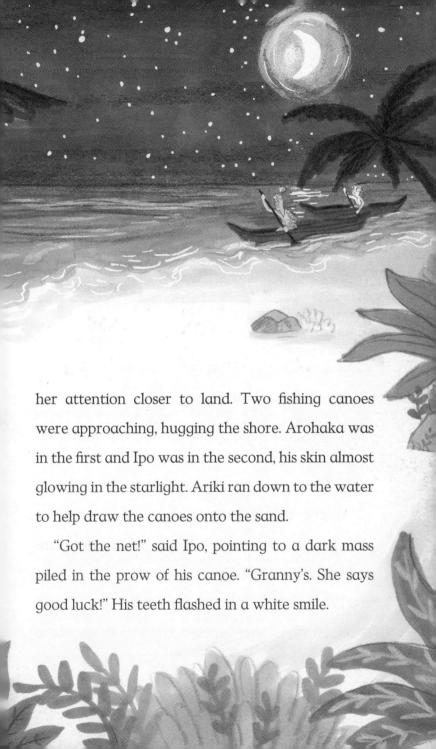

her attention closer to land. Two fishing canoes were approaching, hugging the shore. Arohaka was in the first and Ipo was in the second, his skin almost glowing in the starlight. Ariki ran down to the water to help draw the canoes onto the sand.

"Got the net!" said Ipo, pointing to a dark mass piled in the prow of his canoe. "Granny's. She says good luck!" His teeth flashed in a white smile.

"The boats are Balay's father's – not as fast as mine, but more stable." Arohaka was grinning as well. In the darkness it was almost as if he were a naughty child.

A smattering of running feet announced the arrival of the small pairs of hands.

"I got this many!" Pilo said proudly, holding up his fingers and thumbs all spread out.

"Well, I did say small I suppose!" Arohaka said, looking down at the gang of tots at his feet. He crouched down, bending his creaky knees to be at their height.

"You know who I am, don't you?" he said.

The children nodded with solemn faces.

"You're the grumpy one who argues with the queen!" one of the smallest blurted and was immediately slapped by Pilo.

"That's right. I do argue with the queen," Arohaka said. "She thinks the big shark wants to hurt us. But we know it just wants to have its babies. And that's very special. Tonight is a very special night. And you will do a very special job—"

"We know!" Pilo interrupted.

"Yeah," said a small girl called Heka, who took her thumb out of her mouth to speak, "we seen them pictures in the cave."

"We gonna stop the stripy sharks eatin' the big shark," said another. "We'll hold the net thingy."

Arohaka glanced up at Ipo and Ariki. They shared an astonished moment.

"It seems we should have consulted the Small Hands earlier!" he commented.

"Shall we get in the boats now?" Pilo suggested.

Arohaka unbent. "Well, yes. Yes, let's do that!" They distributed the children by size and strength so each boat would have about equal muscle power. Ipo and Ariki went in one boat with four children and Bad Boy (who refused to be left behind), while

Arohaka went in the other with six, including Pilo who had the most experience on the sea.

Island children were entirely at home in boats, but all the same, the smaller hands were made to sit still and hold on tight while the larger crew did the paddling. As they pushed away from the shore, one of Arohaka's small crew asked, "Why've you got that big spear?"

"Just in case," he replied.

Ariki shuddered. There were so many things that

could go wrong. She counted the heads in each boat,
knowing she would be recounting anxiously many
times before the dawn came.

They made their way round the end of the island.
The stillness of the water made it easy and quick,
but there was something very odd about the state
of the sea.

"It's too still," Ipo said quietly. "I'm more worried
about what the sea's going to do when it 'grows'
than I am about the nihui or your friend Wahine!"

Soon they were on the Turtle Back Beach side of the island, with the darker western sea and sky behind them. Ariki hoped it would hide their silhouettes from anyone who might be awake. As they drew near to the end of the Nose, they began to see nihui fins – crescents of deeper black against the smooth surface.

Arohaka called softly for everyone to bring the canoes together. "It's almost time. We must be ready!"

"We haven't seen the great shark!" Ipo said.

"Wait," said Ariki. "I think my tattoos can tell if she's near."

Ariki leant over the side of the boat. She was usually right-handed, but now she put her left, tattooed arm into the water. At once, the lines and dots began to tingle and the great dark eye of Wahine came into her mind.

"She's here!" Ariki said, smiling. "She's happy we've come."

"Hold the net tight, Small Hands," Arohaka commanded. "Time to protect our friend, the giant shark!"

They lowered the net into the water and held it between the two boats – not a moment too soon.

"Look!" Ipo cried.

There, above the low, dark shape of the sleeping island, the Leaping Dolphin arched in the sky, the three stars of its back just above Manatui's house. And to the north of them, where the Dolphin's eye should be, the comet: burning with yellow fire!

The ocean gave a great sigh. Water rushed away from the reef, leaving its top high and dry, and fish flapping on the exposed coral. The boats and the net between them were sucked further away from the shore, at great speed. Then, just as if the ocean were taking a huge breath in, the water underneath the boat began to rise and rise. It was a wave, a swell of water pushing up and up, moving forward, faster and faster, sweeping them back towards the reef and the channel of the Nose.

The air was filled with a rushing, shushing sound. A froth of white water covered the reef top and the ocean beneath them bulged and rolled. There was no point paddling any more, so all hands, small and large, gripped the net. In front of it, riding the fast-moving wave, was Wahine, her fin and the top of her tail like twin flags sticking out and catching the pale gleam of the Dolphin's new eye. Behind the net were the fins of the nihui, bunched together, held by the power of the water.

The shushing grew to a roar, as boats, shark and net careered with crazy speed towards the reef.

"We'll be smashed to pieces on the coral!" Ipo cried.

"Just hold on!" Arohaka yelled.

Ariki couldn't speak. All she could feel was Wahine's determination, her desperate desire to get into the safety of the lagoon and to release the pups now bursting to be out of her body.

Everyone was screaming, even Arohaka, but just as it looked as if the boats would be broken to firewood and their crew left for the nihui to snack on, the strange bubble-bulge of water reached the Nose. The channel squeezed the wave like a slippery fish, making it shoot up and forward, providing enough water for Wahine to swim through to the lagoon. The net was forced over the end of the Nose. It caught on the coral heads on either side and stretched tight, so the nihui were left outside, snapping their teeth on the drop-off. Wahine was safe in the lagoon!

The sea swirled around them and the canoes bobbed. *Right now,* Ariki thought, *a new generation of giant sharks is beginning.* She tried to remember how many pups the cave pictures had shown, and couldn't. There wasn't time to wonder: the backwash of the

great wave had begun. The boats were pulled back
with such force that they spun out of control, tipping
wildly and washing away from the reef once more.
Ariki and Ipo held on to their boat and as many of

the children as they could reach, but with no hands to hold him Bad Boy was thrown like driftwood. Ariki reached for him but it was too late – the little piglet had gone over the side.

As the boats span on in the whirl of water, Ariki caught sight of Wahine's great dark fin, riding down the middle of the Nose. Her duties as a shark mother were over. With her pups safe in the stillness of the lagoon, she could disappear back into the ocean and would not return in Ariki's lifetime.

CHAPTER 11

The sky was growing light and at last the chaos of water subsided. The two boats rocked gently a short paddle from the reef. Ariki counted heads in both canoes: ten small heads and three bigger ones.

They paddled back towards the Nose. The net no longer covered the entrance to the channel but floated in torn shreds. Ariki gasped when she saw it, afraid that the nihui were in the lagoon feeding on Wahine's pups. But Ipo pointed down into the water where the first light of the day was shining.

"They've found something else to eat," he said.

The growing of the sea had brought huge numbers of groupers, of a kind Ariki had not seen before, into the waters of the drop-off and the nihui were busy eating as many of them as they could.

Pilo called from the other boat.

"Look who we found!" He was holding Bad Boy. "He was swimming over the drop-off."

As they brought their boat closer Ariki could see her guardian's face shining in the dawn light. The old Star Walker looked delighted.

"We have walked the right path," he cried. "We have cared for the great shark, as we care for all our ocean family!"

"What are the warriors of Manna Atta going to say about their wasted journey?" Ipo grinned.

"Wasted?" Arohaka said. "We will celebrate with them and feast on Manatui's breadfruit store and–"

"Not roast piglet!" Ariki added as Bad Boy almost leapt into her arms when Arohaka's boat came alongside. Pilo looked disappointed.

"Don't worry, Small Hands, you will eat well and be rewarded for your help." Arohaka laughed.

Heka pulled at his arm. "Can we go and see the baby giants now?" she asked.

"We can!" he said, smiling more kindly than Ariki had ever seen him smile. "But first I must announce another cause for feasting. Hold our boats steady now, everyone!"

Arohaka reached across and laid his big bony hand on Ariki's head.

"The time has come," he said solemnly, "to celebrate naming my apprentice."

Ariki's heart leapt. She looked up into her guardian's face.

"And I name the gift from the sea, the friend of giant sharks – I name *you*, Ariki!" He sat very

straight in the canoe, his face very still, but Ariki saw the old Star Walker's eyes were as full of tears as her own. Neither of them could speak, but Ipo and the Small Hands had enough voice for them all. As their cheers subsided, a voice piped up.

"*Now* can we go and see the giant shark babies?" Heka wheedled.

Ipo grinned. "Yes!" he cried. "Before the sun gets so high I'm cooked!"

The moment they paddled through the Nose and into the still lagoon they saw them, black against the pale sand. They stared for a long time at the graceful shape of the pups, their mother in miniature. Twenty-five new sharks, beginning a great new cycle for another generation of wondrous giants.

Then all of the children, small and large, Bad Boy the piglet and even the old Star Walker himself went over the side to swim with the shark pups, each one as big as a human.

Ariki floated at the surface and looked down on the babies circling over the white sand of the lagoon. They gave out the same great calm as their mother, and the tattoos on Ariki's body sang as she drew near to the pups, in the same way that they had when she had been close to Wahine.

She swam around, taking in the lovely way they moved and soaking up the peacefulness that filled the lagoon. The skin of their backs was a deep, deep black, so rich and dense it made her want to stroke her fingers from their noses to their tails. But unlike their mother, they were not completely black. From the surface, she caught a flash of something else on their sides. She took a breath and dived down to enjoy the sight of these precious pups from every angle.

What she saw was so amazing she had to swim back to the surface and take a moment to calm

herself before diving again. Each pup had a white blaze on its side, and on that pale background there was a pattern of black dots and stripes, as if the ocean had written a message on each of them. With a swelling heart, Ariki realized that it was the same pattern that she carried on her left arm and leg. Wahine had saved her from the nihui because she recognized her own kind. Somehow these baby giants were connected to the mysterious place that Ariki had come from – her birthplace, lying somewhere far across the sea. One day, when she had become a real Star Walker, she would go and find that place and the people who carried the black-and-white marks of the great Wahine.

But for now, there were sharks to ride.

The warriors from Manna Atta came over the sea chanting about hunting and fighting, and banging their spears on the side of their boats. They expected a great welcome, a forest of spears, people dressed for battle in seashell armour, conches blasting a war cry (and possibly some breakfast). They expected the army of nihui that they'd been told about, and the thrilling, terrifying sight of the murdering demon giant shark, whose size increased every time they talked about it.

But life is seldom what you expect.

What they found was an island steeped in wonder. All along the beach next to the famous Turtle Back lagoon, people stood watching, their children playing in the water; water so still, so clear, that in the early light the children seemed to float in the air. The Queen, Manatui, gave out dishes of breadfruit and then sat hand-in-hand with the venerable old Star Walker in the shallows.

The children were playing an old game, beloved of children in the blue world: riding the tails of shark pups. But these pups were as big as full-grown reef sharks. They swam with a lazy grace that took the breath away, and exuded a kind of peace that made you want to sit in the sand and dream.

And that was what the warriors did. They sat and talked. They watched the sky. They watched the ocean. They forgot about the sharpened spears left lying in the bottom of their boats, and instead paid attention to their lovely world and to each other. They saw the clouds gathering like a shoal of bunching fish and they felt the rain of the new season falling sweetly on their faces.

"Kia orana!" they said to each other. "May you live long!"

COMING SOON!

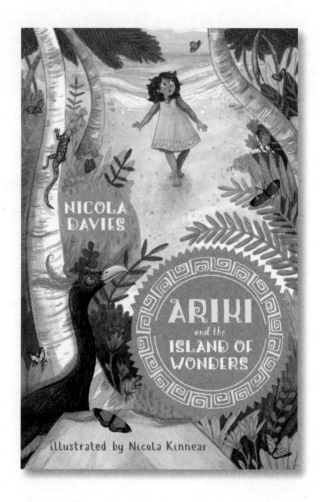

ARIKI
and the
ISLAND OF WONDERS

Ariki and Ipo are making the most of a
beautiful day, sailing the sea near Turtle Island on
a "borrowed" boat. They're too busy daydreaming
to spot the grey clouds gathering overhead – but
then a terrible storm breaks, carrying them miles
from home. After days without food or drink, they
are washed up on an unfamiliar island.

The island is beautiful beyond belief: they see
butterflies, each one lovelier than the last, lizards
chasing across the rocks and, most wonderful of
all, a gigantic blue bird with eyes that glow purple.
When they meet another castaway, however, the
children discover this island is no paradise – there
are dangers lurking in the shadows!